VAMPIRE LOVER

A PURELY PARANORMAL ROMANCE BOOK

C.D. GORRI

Vampire Lover
A Purely Paranormal Romance Book
by C.D. Gorri
Edited by BookNookNuts

Copyright 2020, 2021 C.D. Gorri, NJ

To Tammy! Thank you for everything! Xoxo

STOP! Before you go, sign up for my newsletter and get the latest on my releases, giveaways, freebies and more:
https://www.cdgorri.com/newsletter

This is a work of fiction. All of the characters, names, places, organizations, and events portrayed in this novel are either part of the author's imagination and/or used fictitiously and are not to be construed as real. Any resemblance to any person, living or dead, actual events, locales or organizations is entirely coincidental. This eBook is licensed for your personal enjoyment only. All rights are reserved. No part of this book is to be reproduced, scanned, downloaded, printed, or distributed in any manner whatsoever without written permission from the author. Please do not participate in or encourage piracy of any materials in violation of the author's rights. Thank you for respecting the hard work of this author.

BLURB

Terrence Davies never dreamed he'd be worthy of finding his true mate, then Daisy moves in. Is the sexy normal ready for a Vampire lover?

Daisy Amante just took over the lease on a great apartment in New York City from one of her old boarding school chums. Little does she know her neighbor and landlord is a real live Vampire!

The redheaded hottie tries to hide his sexy good looks behind button down shirts and nerdy looking glasses, but Daisy can see right through his façade. Terrence is something special and she is going to find out what!

Terrence has been sating his Vampire side for years with the bare minimum of blood from specialty butchers, but the second he gets a whiff of his new neighbor he knows there is nothing else that can satisfy his hunger.

He craves Daisy Amante in a way he swore he'd never indulge in again. He tries to fight his urges, but what's a Vampire to do when a sexy curvy goddess knocks on his door in the middle of the night in nothing but her panties?

Can Terrence resist? And will Daisy willingly tie herself to her Vampire lover for eternity?

PROLOGUE

"What the fuck do you mean you're out of wild venison blood?" Terrence growled into his brand-new cell phone as he hustled through the streets of Manhattan towards his apartment building.

It was his third phone this month and from the crunching sound it just made as he squeezed the piece of junk, it would not be his last. Damn things were pretty flimsy when pitted against the strength of a hungry Vampire.

Fucking Chupacabra *sonavabitch* butcher had been his supplier for decades, but now the man was retiring to South America and his idiot son-in-law was in charge. The younger male simply did not understand good service.

"Pietro, I have had a standing order for the past fifty-seven years, why the fuck would you cancel it without checking with me?" He closed his eyes and counted to ten.

Patience, Terrence, you can't kill a man through a cell phone.

"Pietro, just send the goddamned cow blood via special courier tonight. No, it has to be tonight. I have work tomorrow. And if you can't fulfill my future orders, I will have to go through Charlie. You have one more chance, but that's it. Fine. Bye."

He ended the call and ground his teeth together. The cracked screen blinked at him as he hit the little end call button. *Piece of shit.* Another thousand-dollar piece of tech down the drain.

The emptiness in his stomach clawed at him as he hustled to his home. Fuck. He'd gone too long without feeding.

Being a Vampire in the twenty-first century wasn't exactly easy. First off, there were all those pesky wannabes. There was something about sparkly glittering vampires that made his nose twitch.

Second, everyone from the government to the nosy neighborhood cat lady tracked your online orders and any other suspicious activity like bloody hunting dogs. He couldn't feed from the local Vampire Coven's donors. Not since he'd left their ranks after that unpleasant business with his childhood friend.

But how was he supposed to eat for fuck's sake? The world had gotten a lot smaller the more technologically advanced the normals became. Damn he missed the good old days. When people were a lot fewer and farther between.

Still, of all the places in the world, the crowded streets of New York City would always be his home. He turned his head as his supernatural hearing picked up the sounds of the passersby. Everything was normal.

Boring. Busy. But still normal. That was good actually. He could go home and wait for his delivery in peace. Mull over his workday. Make plans for tomorrow. A perfect night.

Terrence thought over the latest musical Pax had delivered to him and his business associate, Broadway hit producer Chance Maddoc. The story was a continuation of the man's previous hit *The Beast of Brooklyn Heights*. Fans and critics had both raved and slammed the writer for leaving the remade Beauty and the Beast fairytale *unfinished*.

Terrence had loved it the way it was, but the

sequel had him chomping at the bit. Leandra, Chance's wife, would keep the female lead of course. Both leads eagerly signed on of course. Terrence would direct them and most of the original cast in this continuation story.

He couldn't wait. The score was original and the lyrics profound. A truly unique telling of things from the Beast's point of view. *Where Beauty Lives* would be the final act in the heart wrenching love story. Oliver Pax still had not shown them the final scene. Preferring to keep the surprise to himself, but that did not matter to Terrence.

Chance had bitched and moaned, even threatened to take away his backing. But Terrence knew him better than that. Chance couldn't walk away from this story any more than he could. It was just that good.

When the last show ended Beauty had left the Beast determined to live her life though she swears her undying love. Heartbroken, the Beast is careless and is taken captive by hunters and madman marauding as scientists. That of course, is the true fear of all supernaturals. Being cut up in a lab underground somewhere.

No wonder they remained in hiding. Shifters, Werewolves, Vampires, Witches and the like.

They'd all vowed to stay hidden from humanity for obvious reasons. Mainly the morons would freak out and want to put every single species under a microscope.

It was far better to stay in the dark. However, as a Vampire who didn't believe in hunting the innocent for his required amount of blood, Terrence had found that ordering specific animal blood from specialty butchers, supernatural ones at that, worked for him.

Jorge, the elder Chupacabra who's butcher shop was located on 182nd Street, had always been reliable. His son-in-law, *Pietro*, was not.

Sigh. It was his own fault for not keeping better track of his blood supply. His hunger gnawed at him, but he ignored it. Auditions went long today. *Where Beauty Lives* was bound to be another hit by Oliver Pax.

There was another one after that in the works as well. A retelling of Hansel and Gretel where the twins were actually a pair of bounty hunters looking for witches and supernatural creatures until Gretel falls in love with a Werewolf.

That would be a good show. Lots of fun and gore. Leandra Madoc had the role of the Witch and a younger unknown would play Gretel, and the up and coming Michael McGregor would play Hansel.

Chance had already signed on to produce the show bringing him three hits in a row if the half-Demon's golden touch stayed true.

Not that Terrence really cared at that moment. He was tired, hungry, and out of sorts. A nice thick steak would serve him well, but he needed blood first. Tonight. Now.

If he couldn't have the venison he preferred, he'd have to wait for the cow blood Pietro had promised would be delivered to his apartment within the hour. He only hoped the idiot remembered to sift it well. Nothing worse than bits of bone and fur in your blood.

Blech. He entered the building and casually took the stairs two at a time. It was an older brick and mortar construct, but one of his favorites.

Rent controlled. Busy, but clean part of town. He'd bought it at the turn of the last century because he'd liked the location. It suited him these days to play the landlord while he busied himself with directing.

The excitement of Broadway still captivated him at every turn. Whenever he began a new project, he always felt the thrill of starting all over again. Terrence was settled in his routine.

Not a lot could surprise a man with a few centuries under his belt, he supposed. Directing had come rather easily to him. He took it up after decades of people watching from his hiding place in the shadows.

Because of their long lifespans, Vampires were often thought of to be immortal. Some were, or as close to it as possible, he figured. But he was only three hundred twenty-seven years old. Young for his kind.

All sorts of lore about Vampires existed in the world. Each one telling their own version of what they believed Vampires to be. Dark masters, the undead, cold and unfeeling, bloodsucking fiends basically. *Sigh.*

The best description he'd ever heard had come from his great-grandfather after a young and thoughtful Terrence had raised the question at the tender age of nine of whether or not he was human.

"We are not the undead, my boy," he said and squeezed Terrence's tiny hand in his old withered one, *"Vampirism is more a mutation than a disease. So yes, we are human. But we are also so much more. Our*

longevity gives us an ability to feel more compassion for the briefly alive humans than they could ever feel for themselves. And when you are older, my boy, should you find your mate amongst them, may you give the gift of life to your chosen so that you can enjoy the centuries together as I and your grandmother have these past five-hundred years."

But there would be no mate for him. He'd locked up his heart a long time ago.

It was better that way.

CHAPTER ONE

Terrence slowed his pace as he arrived at his floor. There was a banging noise coming from somewhere, but for some reason it didn't alarm him.

"Ah, the penthouse," he smirked as he stopped in front of his midnight blue door.

He didn't mind not having an elevator. Vampires had stores of energy. Super strength, superior health, prolonged youthful appearance, you name it. Well, Leandra certainly didn't miss the daily jogs up all those stairs to her former little apartment that shared the floor with his. She told him that little bit daily. But he didn't mind it. Not at all.

He missed having her as a neighbor though. He

liked her company, but he was profoundly happy for her and Chance. The half-Demon had found his true mate in Terrence's songbird neighbor for which Terrence accepted all responsibility.

He did introduce them after all. For that they should name at least one of their offspring after him. Or so he told them both frequently.

A mate. What a wondrous thing indeed. Not that he'd ever have cause to worry about that. He would never take a mate. Not after what he'd seen and done. He didn't deserve one.

Terrence exhaled, pushing the sad thought from his mind. He removed his key from his pocket and growled loudly. What the heck was going on? He could barely think with all the incessant banging coming from down the hall.

Oh. Right. He'd forgotten that it was the first of the month. *Moving day.* The holidays had come and gone again with no real impact on him or his schedule. But it was February first and he had a new tenant and neighbor.

Some former school chum of Leandra's. Well, he would save the introductions for another time. He was borderline *hangry* and that was not something anyone wanted to be around. Especially not when meeting a Vampire for the first time.

"Ow! Dammit!" The sound of a woman's screech met his ears and he sighed heavily.

He couldn't very well ignore it if some poor normal was hurt on his watch. Maybe she'd seen a mouse or something. He waited a beat just to see if she was okay. Then came the crash and a second scream.

Shit. Terrence took off down the hall.

The door to Leandra's old apartment was open and inside he saw a woman barely hanging on to a ladder in the middle of the crowded living room. She must have been trying to hang something to the ceiling, but from the looks of things, without any success.

He surmised she missed the nail because of the way she was holding her thumb to her rather ample chest. Her wealth of chestnut colored hair was tied behind her head revealing a pleasant oval shaped face. Her clothes were comfortable for moving day, just jeans and a cotton shirt. Nothing outrageously sexy or alluring, but for some reason he could not stop staring at her.

She was petite he supposed, and curvy as hell. Pretty and young, the woman had clear, smooth ivory skin and large pale green eyes.

She cursed like a sailor as she held her bruised

hand and even did a little dance while she stood precariously on the ladder. But that wasn't what had Terrence freezing in his steps.

No. It was her scent. Freshly fallen rain, clean, cut grass, with just a hint of wild herbs. He could identify sage, thyme, lavender, and rosemary as he inhaled another breath, sucking her fragrance deep inside of him to savor and store.

Each note of her fragrance was unique, just like her. With every moment that passed he found himself memorizing more of her. This strange woman who had suddenly captivated him.

Yes, his senses were all supernaturally enhanced, but for the moment they were fucking useless. He was frozen like a damn statue. It was true that Vampires were on average stronger, faster, and generally healthier than most normals.

But none of that explained why his heart thudded in his chest like he'd just run a marathon. Neither could it justify why his breathing grew rushed like he'd just emerged from being held under water for far too long. His eyes stung. His stomach clenched. His muscles tensed. What the fuck was going on?

He barely had time to check himself as his fangs burst through his gums and his claws extended from his fingertips. Shit. This was not good.

Unlike his friends Chance and Oliver, Terrence's physical changes when his Vampire side wanted out were minimal but still frightening to the average normal. Also unlike them, there was no *other voice* inside his head. No other persona that he shared his soul with. It was just Terrence. He was *Vampire*.

Kind of human, but more. A mutation discovered centuries before had divided the species. Vampires were stronger, lived longer, and also drank blood to remain healthy and virile. But they were also always in control. He made the decisions. Some things were biological, but others were made by choice.

Occasionally, the long life of a Vampire became too much for the individual and he or she would lose all semblance of humanity with the aid of a Dark Witch or Warlock. Becoming Hunter Vampires, little better than rabid dogs who heeled to their dark masters. Terrence hated the very idea of them, though more was being done by his kind to reverse the condition.

Then there were even darker aspects of Vampirism. Individuals who would use humans as cattle, who cared nothing for other forms of life. These elitists were called *Revenants*. Odd that the word be so close to *reverent* when these creatures revered nothing but themselves.

Terrence shuddered. He had personal knowledge of Revenants. It filled him with revulsion just thinking about the tragedy from his past. It was in fact the very reason he vowed to always be alone in the world. And yet every fiber of his being was pushing him to forget he'd ever made such a foolish promise to himself.

He had no excuse. He was not a Shifter. He could control himself. Despite his grandfather's lessons on mates Terrence knew he had the power to walk away.

It was just him and him alone. He had no excuse for wanting to break his vow to remain alone for the rest of his days. Never once had he been tempted to try and find a companion.

Except for at that very moment. Right then, everything inside of him was screaming one word above all others.

His blood coursed through his veins faster than a bullet train. The sound like roaring thunder in his ears. He didn't blink. Could hardly move. The woman finally realized she was not alone. Big green eyes stopped and stared at him. Her pink mouth hung open, the pain in her finger momentarily forgotten.

Terrence's entire body went still as the object of his focus turned to view him. His muscles tightened, cock hardened, and throat burned in response.

He opened his mouth and said the only thing he was able to in a voice that was barely more than a growl.

"Mate."

CHAPTER TWO

Well, shit, Daisy huffed another breath as she climbed the ladder and attempted to reattach the plant hook to the ceiling. *Again.*

Sigh. Chubby girls did not do ladders. Even if they were fairly active. And she was. As much as a girl with her condition could be. Besides, even if chubby girls did go around running up and down ladders, they didn't do it well.

As for why she was standing on the rickety old step ladder she'd found in the broom closet, that was easy. Daisy loved plants. And this particular vine was one of her favorites.

She'd had it for years and years. It had been with her since boarding school. When the hook had given way and it came crashing down from the ceiling, she almost died trying to catch it. Good news, the plant survived, bad news, the hook came down with it.

Still, she was glad she'd managed to save the poor beauty. Even if she did lose the pot. That was okay. She had dozens of empties at the moment.

It was a good thing she'd started making her own with the way she went through them. *LOL.* Anyway it was a great outlet for her creativity. Once she'd started with plants, she'd learned that a lot of the more efficient planters were simply too expensive for her to keep up with.

So, she began to make them herself. Nowadays her pottery was a permanent part of her catalog on *Daisy's Garden*. That was what she called her online store.

New York was too expensive for her to rent space. She sold her plants and several of her affordable handcrafted pots to several local flower shops. She did most of her business on her own online store and was hoping to grow her local customers now that she lived in the area.

Daisy loved the city. She'd always dreamed of living in the Big Apple ever since she was a kid in Pennsylvania. Having no money except for a small inheritance from her grandmother had made her weary of the sky-high rents. As a result, she'd been commuting from New Jersey every day to make her deliveries. It was hell on her second-hand commercial van not to mention her wallet.

Imagine her surprise when a friend from her old boarding school, *Mrs. Parker's School for Girls*, Leandra Katell, had messaged her with the news that she was getting married. The two of them had spent a good amount of time together in those days.

Daisy's father travelled a lot for work and her mother had been unable to care for their shy, awkward, and often ill teenager. She'd been shipped off to the secluded school where she pretty much stayed to herself.

Except for Leandra, she hardly talked to anyone. Though the other woman had two best friends, Daisy had always felt drawn to her. She was so happy and outgoing, comfortable in her own skin.

Everything Daisy wanted to be. She smiled at the memories of her time back then. She'd been chubby and awkward. Her health was always a problem, but Leandra had made her laugh time and again with her outrageous antics. They'd spent most of their physical education classes hiding from their teacher while Daisy dreamt of gardens and Leandra of singing.

Well, her old chum had certainly hit it big. And on Broadway of all places! Her hit musical, the *Beast of Brooklyn Heights*, was the talk of the town. Not only that, but she'd fallen in love with the show's producer! Her life had turned into a real fairytale! *Sigh.*

If only mine could turn out that way, she mused. But in a way it had. Leandra had been looking for someone to take-over her lease in the heart of Manhattan and Daisy had, of course, jumped at the opportunity.

It warmed her heart that Leandra even thought about her in the middle of her own happiness. Daisy sighed loudly. Apartment 6J wasn't exactly big, but it was hers now. Located on the top floor of one of those old ten-story buildings that were almost non-existent these days.

The place had character. Real brick on the outside, old marble tile in the entryway. The hallways were painted a dark blue with white tiled floors. There was no elevator of course, but her thighs would thank her later. At least that was what she told herself time and again.

The apartment was small, but big enough for her. She had access to the rooftop where she'd been assured, she could set up her small kiln and greenhouse. That had been the first thing she'd asked and could have danced for joy when Leandra had told her it was no problem at all. Best of all it was rent controlled!

The movers had already finished setting stuff up on the roof for her. Now she just had to get things organized. It was amazing that what a few extra bucks couldn't do, a flash of her big green eyes could.

She had practically begged the moving men to climb the extra stairs and set up for her. She'd offered them money, and they still refused. But when she'd asked them in for a cup of coffee and some grilled cheese sandwiches, a joke, and a smile, they not only carried everything to the roof, they took an hour to set it all up.

What a great bunch of guys! She looked at the card with the tallest one's number on it and giggled. She'd given him a small houseplant for his mom and he gave her his number. Picking up phone numbers from virtual strangers was not a common occurrence for Daisy. She would more than likely lose it before she used it, but it was a great compliment at any rate.

She'd always been so shy around men in her younger days. Certain they wouldn't notice a chubby little thing like her. Nearing thirty had definitely changed her. Daisy figured it was long past time she felt comfortable in her own skin.

Her health was better than it had been in years. After her grandmother passed and she'd been given her own initial diagnosis, she learned that life was precious. And short.

There were no guarantees. Her parents had reacted to the news that their daughter had a heart defect by pushing her away and sending her off to school. It had hurt at first, but she understood now it was their problem, not hers.

She was not going to let anyone else ever dictate her self-worth again. She finished school with high marks, took her small legacy her grandmother had left her, and started her own business. After working for years to get her company off the ground, she'd finally decided to work on herself.

She had a new haircut, some new clothes, and now a new apartment to go with her new attitude. Daisy was more than ready to take Manhattan by storm. But first, she had to take care of her babies and make sure they were okay.

Her "babies" being the four or five dozen or so plants, miniature trees, and flowers she kept in her apartment at all times. With the thermometer set at a comfortable seventy-degrees Fahrenheit and the cool mist humidifier going, she'd have the place up to par in no time.

If only she could get this dang hook to stay. She'd tried to use a bigger screw instead of the one it came in. Hoping to bully the thing into staying up she tried everything to jimmy it into place, but she'd only managed to get it stuck.

Desperate to finish the little project, Daisy had grabbed a hammer thinking she'd pound the screw in the rest of the way, only she missed. The screw that is, not her finger. That she of course got. *Ouch.*

"Ow! Dammit!"

She yelped and dropped the tools, cradling her hand to her chest. Daisy groaned not even reacting to the sound of footsteps coming towards her. They grew louder and faster.

Great. Someone else to witness her humiliation. She turned around carefully from her position on top of the ladder and almost lost her footing. If the pain in her hand wasn't so intense, she'd have thought she dropped dead and was in the presence of an angel. The stranger was absolutely beautiful.

Yes, she thought, *men could be beautiful.* He was proof. The tall, sexy as hell man was not just drop-dead gorgeous. He was also staring at her like she was the all-you-can-eat shrimp fest at Red Lobster and he was starved.

She took in his appearance from the sedate checkered button-down he wore tucked into a pair of tight khakis, all the way down to his evenly laced shockingly orange suede sneakers. A black-banded smart watch was strapped around his left wrist, but other than that he wore no jewelry.

He was just the kind of guy she'd always secretly lusted after. Sort of *nerd chic*, she supposed. So much yumminess wrapped up in a button-down. Of course, she'd never seen so much muscle in such oddly un-macho clothing.

Whatever. It worked. Daisy practically drooled on herself. He was just so darn hot. She even forgot about her poor abused appendage while she stared at him. She felt too warm all of a sudden, and truth be told, a little wet in certain places. And, *gulp*, was he staring also?

"Sorry. Um, sorry was I too loud?" she felt her cheeks flame.

Embarrassment warred with attraction as she moved carefully down the ladder. Daisy extended her uninjured hand but put it quickly down as the handsome stranger remained still and silent by her door.

"You alright?" She asked concerned that he might have had a stroke or something.

"You hurt your hand," he stated in a deeply masculine voice that sent tendrils of awareness shooting down her spine.

Daisy had never experienced anything like it. She swallowed hard. Looking down at her still throbbing thumb, she frowned. Darn it. She was definitely going to have a black and blue by morning.

"Crap, I better get some ice. Oh no, I don't have any," she sighed and closed her eyes.

"I'll get you some," he said and before she could blink he was gone.

That was weird. Well, it certainly was the fastest she'd ever managed to run off a hot guy. At least she'd have some fodder for her fantasies later on. *Sigh.*

She walked over to the second-hand couch Leandra had left in the apartment which Daisy promptly claimed as her own and sat down gingerly. Moving in was hard work. She was used to being on her feet for long periods at a time, but carrying heavy boxes and unpacking added to the strain on her muscles.

Now this. Ugh. She sighed again and looked at her quickly blackening thumb. No sooner had she inhaled another breath than the sexy stranger was back.

"Here," he moved close to her and took her hand in his own large, callused one. Ooh, she hadn't expected that. Figured he'd be smooth and polished but clearly he had a hobby where he worked with his hands.

Not that she knew what he did for a living, but construction did not come to mind based on his attire. Then again, his muscles told another story.

Ooh. A mystery man, she thought to herself. When was the last time she enjoyed a game of twenty questions with a member of the opposite sex?

Far too long, was her sadly accurate answer. But that didn't matter she realized as she took in his sharp, aristocratic features and pale as moonlight skin.

She would gladly play with him. *Heck yeah.* She found him positively captivating. So good looking, it hurt to stare at him for too long. But she didn't want to blink, she was afraid he'd vanish. A perfect figment of her imagination.

He had angular features, that should have been sharp, but only made him more masculine. His hair was a sort of pale red. More strawberry blonde than Ron Weasley carrot red.

She liked it. A lot. Especially when his gray eyes met hers. Daisy had to bite her tongue to stop from gasping aloud. Holy crap. She'd never seen eyes like that. They glittered like molten steel. Hard and honest, but at the same time hot enough to brand her with his gaze.

Gulp.

He took her hand and laid a thin towel on top followed by a plastic baggie full of crushed ice. Immediate relief flowed through her and she sighed gratefully.

"Thank you, Mister? I'm sorry, I don't know your name," she smiled hoping to lighten the mood and cover up her bizarre attraction to the stranger.

"I have to go," he seemed to whisper the words even as his head drifted closer to her.

OMG! Was he going to kiss her? She wanted him to, she realized with a start. Daisy leaned in closer, unable to help herself. She swore she heard something. A deep rumble coming from him.

He seemed to groan, then just like that he was gone. *Poof!* Like he'd never existed. She stood mouth open for a full minute at his hasty exit.

"Guess you scared him off with your sexy smile," she laughed at herself and shook her head.

Too bad, she thought. He was cute, but obviously mental. Oh well. Back to work.

CHAPTER THREE

It had been three days. Three days since he'd seen her. Ever since then her sweet and fresh garden scent seemed to haunt his every move. Three days since the last time he'd managed a single coherent thought.

Terrence entered his apartment quickly after work and immediately turned on the stereo. He couldn't risk hearing her. Scenting her was bad enough. He'd been walking around with a semi-erection for days now. A little Mozart might help. Classical music was good for the soul now and then, or so he'd heard.

Fuck it. He was willing to try anything at this point. And after a day of listening to people sing, he appreciated the instrumental strains as they sounded through his set of high-end Bose speakers.

"Better," he mused while he started to gather up his discarded clothes to run a load of laundry.

Next, he loaded soiled dishes and glasses into the dishwasher. Then after spraying and wiping every available surface clean, he finally sat down on the couch. Hints of lavender and sage seemed to find him through the very walls they shared.

He recalled the lovely oval face of his new neighbor. Her pale skin, pink lips, chestnut hair, and incredible green eyes imbedded in is brain like any well learned lesson from his youth. She was so beautiful. So unattainable.

Mine, his brain roared. No. He would never claim her. And yet, he could not stop thinking about her.

Dammit. He was restless. What else could he do to distract himself from his sexy new neighbor?

Clean until you pass out. He got out his Dyson and moved the coffee table to the side of the room. After vacuuming the bare floors and rearranging the furniture, he decided enough was enough.

It was Friday night. Late at that. She was probably out with her friends. Or with a man. No. He didn't even want to think about the possibility.

Muscles bunched he closed his eyes. *Maybe she's asleep.*

Yes, that worked. He could picture her in bed. Alone. Safe from him. Safe from temptation.

Of course, picturing her in bed did nothing to relieve the hard-on that was currently popping a tent in his sweats.

Inhale. And exhale. Nope. Still there.

Fuck. Maybe it was time for a little dinner? Nah. His stomach revolted at the thought of food.

Blood? Ugh. The idea of imbibing animal blood at that moment left him feeling worse than the idea of food.

When in doubt, Pop-Tarts. He smirked as he headed over to the pantry. He always kept a wide variety of the crunchy, gooey sweetness on hand. They weren't really food. More like an edible addiction.

Like my mate. Fuck. No sooner had the thought entered his mind then there was a knock at the door. Who the heck could that be? With all the cleaning products in the air his nose could barely detect whether the person was human or not.

Sniff. Uh oh.

His dick was undeniably hard and *she* was here. Right outside his door. Terrence took a second and pulled his t-shirt down to cover the damn thing, but she was pounding away furiously.

What the heck? He didn't sense anyone else in the hallway. She was alone. So what was the hurry?

Terrence answered the door with half a strawberry Pop-Tart sticking out of his mouth and the box held precariously in front of his throbbing dick.

Holy shit. Said box hit the floor when he saw her.

"Let me in quick!" She squeaked and ran past him.

His new neighbor sported nothing but a blue polka-dotted thong as she hustled past Terrence and ducked behind his couch, giving him an incredible view of her heart shaped ass before she crouched out of sight.

"Towel?"

"What?" he said with his mouth still full.

"Do you have a towel or something?"

"Uh yeah. Hang on," he reached for the throw blanket he kept on the chair and tossed it at her swallowing the suddenly dry toaster pastry.

One side of his mouth quirked up as he imagined what the heck mess she'd gotten into now. As if the hammer and thumb thing was more common than not. The woman in question sighed in relief before she appeared, stepping out from behind his furniture.

The loosely knit afghan had holes between the knots giving him tantalizing glimpses of her pale flesh between the beige yarn. He didn't want to come off as some sort of deranged pervert, so he managed to stop himself from staring. Barely.

"So, uh, I understand you are the landlord?" She asked as if it were perfectly acceptable to come barreling into one's landlord's apartment in nothing but your underwear in the middle of the night.

"Um, yeah, that's right."

"We, uh, weren't properly introduced the other day. My name is Daisy Amante."

"Terrence. Davies. Terrence Davies."

"The director? No shit," she said and he struggled not to laugh.

There she stood looking outrageously cute in practically nothing and she was chatting like they were at a tea party. Didn't she know she was practically offering herself to him? Teasing him like a red flag in front of a bull?

Nope. She had no idea, he realized. She wasn't

flirty or seductive. She was, *sniff*, embarrassed, he realized as he inhaled her scent gaining her emotions from the tiny whiff. How could one woman be so interesting and exasperating at the same time?

"Forgive me, Ms. Amante, but why are you here? And why are you, uh, naked?"

"Oh that, well, I am wearing underwear," she pointed out.

"Barely," he disagreed. The picture of her bare ass would be forever etched into his mind. Wouldn't he love a nibble?

Yes.

No.

Agh. Focus. He forced himself to stop thinking of her ass and to start listening to what she was saying. Which was what again? Oh.

"Well, you see," she looked down and bit her lip, a habit he found endearing, before continuing, "I stepped into the hallway with my robe on to grab a delivery. For some reason the man put it against the opposite wall-"

"Yeah, they do that here," he interrupted and offered her his other half of Pop-Tart since she was now staring at it.

"Thanks. I love strawberry," she sighed as she

bit into the pastry and his dick went up again. Like a fucking flagpole.

"So?" He nodded waiting for her to continue. The quicker he heard her tale, the quicker she could leave and he could forget his dilemma.

Claim her or leave town. Fucking shit.

"Sorry. Okay, so the door shut and locked when I went to get the package, and my robe got stuck. I tried yelling, but your music was on loud. So I, uh, decided to risk it."

She shrugged and her cheeks burned a bright pink. Damn she was cute.

"I take it you are locked out?"

"Yep."

"Let me grab some things."

"Okie dokie," she said and moved to follow him.

Each step brought more of her sun-warmed grassy fresh fragrance into his nostrils. Fuck he wanted to roll around in her, like a puppy on a summer lawn.

Nope. That simply wouldn't do.

"Uh, you wait here," Terrence said.

"Thanks," she shrugged and sank down onto the sofa.

For a second Terrence couldn't move. The

woman was sitting practically bare-assed on his couch. If possible, his dick grew even harder. Was it normal to be jealous of a sofa? Probably not. Fuck. He was so screwed.

Terrence turned quickly. He took shallow breaths as he went to the kitchen to grab his toolbox from under the sink. The more time he spent around her the more difficult it was to keep his baser instincts in check.

"I'll be back in a few minutes. Please make yourself at home."

No. Don't. Please don't touch anything. I'll never get your scent out of my apartment. I'll probably sneak over and bite you in the middle of the fucking night. Hell, as it is I am going to go home and bury my face in the couch hoping to smell you there. I can't wait to nibble your neck. Your pussy. Every delectable inch. I want you. Mate. Mine.

"Shit. I am fucked," he mumbled as he walked down the hall.

He turned his brain off as he scooped her package from the floor and turned to her locked door. Her bright crimson robe was there. Stuck in the locked door like she'd said. Not that he doubted her at all. It was just unfair. Why the hell would Fate send him a mate? Him of all people?

And why such a cute one at that? She was damn near irresistible. Still, he had to try. For her sake and his. He just had to get her door unlocked then he could go back home. Alone.

After a few minutes he had it open. He set the package down on her table and took a moment to look around. The place was amazing. An actual garden in the middle of a brick, steel, and mortar city. Who knew things like this existed?

He could practically feel the care she felt for her plants in the room. And she'd only been there a few days. Imagine what it would be like a month, a year, ten years from now! His keen senses were already able to discern her compassion, her focus, and the total pleasure she felt at growing things.

A woman with the capacity to love like that was a rare thing. Rare and sweet and deserving of so much more than he was. So much more than he had left to give.

What was he anyway except a fool? Terrence could not trust himself to take care of her the way she deserved.

After all, he thought he could change Eric. Thought he could save his boyhood friend from heading down the wrong path. But he'd been wrong.

He had never been able to persuade his friend to follow the rules. Eric was wild and brash. He'd believed normals were little more than cattle or prizes in a game.

Terrence had hardly recognized him when the local Coven had carted him off to be tried and later imprisoned. Revenants were granted mercy in the form of life in the bleak, lonely, and magically reinforced cells that served as their prisons for as long as they lived. Which could be pretty fucking long.

The Guardians who watched over the hated place were loyal men and women who practiced secret, sacred magic. They were the only supernaturals who knew how to keep a Vampire or Revenant securely away from society.

So many secrets. Terrence could never burden a sweet woman like Daisy with all the hidden mysteries of his kind. Vampires trusted no one. None in the entire universe.

That was why they still clung to and supported all those myths about being undead, allergic to sunlight and garlic, of having no souls. Nothing but nonsense. Vampires were very much alive.

But how could he tell her that it was a mutation that occurred somewhere thousands of years ago that split the human race into several subspecies? How could he expect her to believe there were Shifters, Werewolves, those mixed with blood of the Fae, Demons, Angels, and of course Vampires?

He had no means of support now. No one to help protect her from his enemies and yes, he had them. Still, even after he left the Coven following Eric's capture, Terrence was bound to keep their ways secret. And still, there was one person he could tell. One person by law. His fated mate.

For that was the only way he could share with her his Vampiric mutation. Thereby granting her a life that was practically immortal. Ensuring they would be together for all eternity.

His blood pumped through his veins at the thought of having that. Of having his mate. Of being a pair instead of a lone solitary figure. So tempting. So very tempting indeed. But could he do that? Did he deserve happiness?

These were not easy questions to answer. He shook his head, picked up her robe and headed back to his apartment where she sat waiting.

Naked. His brain added the almost forgotten fact and he groaned out loud. That was it. He needed her out of the apartment so he could think.

And maybe masturbate.

"All done," he said with false brightness as he entered the room.

Fuck me, he thought as she stood up briefly flashing him in the process.

He held out her robe and she squeaked happily as she tugged it on. She turned her back to him and dropped the blanket, bending down to retrieve it from the floor.

Gulp.

"Your place is immaculate! I had no idea guys could clean like that! Next time you are in the mood, come on over," she laughed and handed him the still warm afghan seemingly unaware of the double meaning of her invitation. *Gulp.*

He just nodded and walked her to the door. Closing it behind her with a wave. He tried not to breathe too deeply but he knew he was screwed.

Her flowery scent hung in the air reminding him of her bountiful beauty. His tongue salivated. Cock pulsed. Thirst like he'd never felt before burned his throat as his fangs pierced his gums.

Terrence swallowed hard as he stood up and went to the fridge. He grabbed the emergency vial of O-positive that he'd kept deep in the freezer for near on five years. Fuck, but he needed it now. Needed to control his thirst before he did something unforgiveable. After running it under warm water he swallowed the contents.

It stung as it slid down his throat. His body reveling in the nutrition the lifegiving fluid provided while his mind rejected the origin. It craved his mate and no one else.

Still, Terrence hissed and sighed as he felt his muscles strengthen and his mind sharpen. A Vampire needed blood to live. It was simple as that.

Not so simple was living next to his mate and not claiming her. He would need the added control the human blood would bring if he was going to succeed until he made his choice.

Claim his mate or let her go?

CHAPTER FOUR

Daisy. Her name is Daisy, Terrence replayed the scene in his head again and again as he headed to the theatre the next day.

What an ass he'd been! Rather than fumble for words, he'd chosen silence as his shield. She must think he was nuts!

He couldn't get over the way she'd changed the place. The apartment he'd known for decades that had most recently been inhabited by Leandra was now barely recognizable.

When he'd stepped inside, he felt as if he'd been transported somewhere else. Somewhere as green as the emerald flames he'd seen in her eyes. Like he was stepping out of time to a place he felt safe and warm.

Plants, flowers and shrubs had taken up every inch of bare space. Where Leandra hung brightly colored vintage curtains from every window, Daisy had stripped them all away. Replacing fabric with the natural greenery of her plants. Choosing sunlight instead of darkness.

Ironic that his kind was rumored to perish in the sun. It was quite the contrary. Terrence was a little fair-skinned but that was because of his English heritage as opposed to any deathly allergy. Daisy was even more pale than he. A wonder since he would bet his life on her loving the outdoors.

Her home was a veritable garden. Long draping vines, spiky little succulents, delicate orchids, blooming cacti, miniature roses, potted trees that looked part of a tropical island and so many more. He could hardly take them all in. She'd managed to create a paradise inside the tiny barely 800 square foot space.

It was breathtaking, beautiful, but nothing compared to the curvy goddess who had stood dead center of it all on a ladder the first time he'd spied her.

More like a pillar, he thought dreamily picturing

his beautiful torment. So wrapped up in the image inside his brain Terrence almost walked into Chance.

That's what he got for daydreaming about his new neighbor. But damn, she was like a bloody miracle. His miracle. Gods how he wanted her. So very badly. More with each passing minute.

He skirted around the amused looking Chance. Not bothering to respond to his friend's taunting laughter. He could be the butt of his joke. It mattered very little to him these days. Nothing mattered, except *her*.

"Watch out, Terr!" Shouted Leandra, but her warning came too late.

He'd been so wrapped up in conjuring images of the sexy little sprite next door in her work jeans and loose cotton shirt that he'd walked right off the stage missing the staircase entirely.

Thank fuck for Vampire reflexes. Terrence managed to crouch as he fell. Turning what should have been a catastrophe into a rather acrobatic tumble and finally, into a standing position with relatively little harm done to his person.

"Geez, dude, what's gotten into you?" Leandra called, running down the stairs to catch up with him. Chance was right there too on her heels. As always.

Only now Terrence understood why the half-Demon felt compelled to be near his mate at every moment. He had hardly spoken to Daisy and she filled his every thought. What would life be like if he claimed her? How would he get anything done?

Who cared? As long as he had her everything would be fine. His thirst would be quenched and the awful hunger sated. *Finally.*

"Shit, Terrence, you need to supplement that butcher blood you buy with some of the real stuff already!" Chance growled at him.

Of course, his buddy would assume it was his choice of diet that was at fault for his clumsiness. Terrence blinked slowly. Once then again.

"My diet is fine, Chance. Thank you for your concern, Lea," he said choosing to speak to his friend's mate.

Yes, he was stalling. He wasn't sure he wanted to share the good news just yet. Heck. He didn't even know if it was good news.

Hadn't he vowed never to take a mate? Of course, when he made that vow, he never thought he would actually meet the fantastic creature designed by the universe to be his and his alone.

The only person in creation who could satisfy his inner cravings and make him whole. It was certainly a bonus that she was beyond beautiful and that body of hers made him want to kneel down and beg.

She was it for him. All the half-naked dancers he saw daily couldn't even raise his blood pressure. But daisy in muddy jeans and a t-shirt. Hot damn. That was something special.

She was something special. His *sete di cuore*. The Vampire name was more than a term of endearment. It was a saying from the old country of his particular Coven. Mostly Italians and the odd English and Irish Vampire in the early days of New York City.

Sete di cuore indeed. It meant that Daisy was the only one for him. The sole person in the universe that his heart thirsted for. She was his other half. His mate for eternity.

If he bit her and she accepted his claim she could be. Mine forever.

Of course, if he were to solidify the tentative bond that had already started to form between them, his heart would no longer be his own. It would be hers entirely. She would become his reason for being.

The thought scared and intrigued him all at the same time. Given his past, would Terrence ever truly be able to give of himself so completely?

His phone rang and he looked down at the thing. The number was unknown so he ignored it. Probably a spam call. It didn't matter. Not when his future was at stake here.

Poor choice of words, he grimaced. Vampires and stakes of any kind were not good combinations. Besides, so what if he'd failed at his childhood friend. Eric had become a monster. A Revenant in both deed and design.

"Is she important to you Terrence?" Leandra interrupted his musings.

"I don't know what you mean," he lied.

"Terr," Chance turned to him, black eyes glowing with his Demon, "I know about your concerns. Just remember that was his choice, not yours. You deserve happiness, old friend."

"What are you talking about?" Leandra asked.

"Nothing, love. It is his business," Chance said and nodded to Terrence who reminded himself at that moment that these were what real friends looked like.

Leandra with her soft caring eyes and Chance there to support him no matter what. Though the pain of his former friend's fate still ached inside of him, maybe it was time to let it go?

Eric had been all too fond of ill-gotten human blood. Vampire Covens existed for the reason of providing aid in times of *sete empia*. The unholy thirst that plagued his kind. But theirs had failed to contain Eric's bloodlust.

Lost in his memories Terrence barley heard Chance calling his name once more until the half-Demon tapped him on the forehead. *Hard.*

"You with us buddy?" Chance waved his hand in front of Terrence's face. The Vampire slapped it away and sighed.

"Knock it off. Look, there is something I need to tell both of you about my new neighbor," he began.

"Who, Daisy? Isn't she great?" Leandra bit her lip and grinned wickedly.

"Yes. She is here-"

"And did you see all her plants? Crazy right? I mean the girl has got one heck of a green thumb. I hope you don't mind I told her she could have a section of the roof for her kiln and greenhouse. That was okay, right?"

One after the other, Leandra's ramblings helped paint a picture of the woman who was currently occupying every inch of Terrence's mind. Chance smiled indulgently at his wife before interrupting.

"Angel, why don't we let Terrence finish?"

"What? Oh. My bad," she giggled and tucked herself into her mate's side.

Terrence found himself wishing Daisy were there with him and that he had any right to hold her like that. To lay claim to the sweet normal who was probably puttering around on the rooftop with her plants. He smiled for a second, then fear spiked through his blood.

The rooftop? This was Manhattan and that building was ten stories high! He hadn't been up there in months. Anything could have happened to make it unsafe or structurally unsound.

"Shit," he muttered and grabbed his keys before taking off at inhuman speeds.

"Terr?" Chance called his name, but Terrence couldn't spare the time.

"What did I say?" Leandra asked.

"Uh, I think he's gone to check on your friend," Chance answered his wife.

No, Terrence thought, *I've gone to check on my mate.*

Mine. The word felt good and right as images of

Daisy with her shoulder length chestnut brown hair and her big green eyes. So fresh and beautiful, sweet as the scent of flowers and clean soil that clung to her.

She should be safe and warm, inside, against the bitter February winds that attacked Terrence's scarf and hat as he rushed down the street. But no, at that particular moment, she could very well be in danger!

The thought horrified him while spurring him on faster. He usually did not use his superhuman abilities in broad daylight, but what choice did he have? None as far as he could see.

Finally, he reached the building and took the stairs four at a time. He passed her apartment door, listening for any signs of her inside, but there were none. Disappointment warred with anxiety as he feared the worst. She was on the roof. In bitter cold weather with high winds due from the impending winter storm.

As he neared the last staircase a crash sounded from overhead. Terrence's heart stopped. Without a moment's thought he tore up the fifteen steps that led to the rooftop and ripped the door clean off the hinges.

"Daisy!"

"Over here," came the sweet voice he'd been longing to hear again ever since he woke up that morning.

Terrence zeroed in on the direction the sound was coming from and nearly lost his mind. Daisy was standing far too close to the roof's edge trying to push a large barrel filled with what looked like dirt to the edge. At her feet were the remnants of what used to be an enormous ceramic pot. There were boxes and crates stacked on the flat black roof next to a newly erected miniature greenhouse.

"What are you doing?" He growled the question and in two steps had her plastered to his side.

"Oof," she yelped and he loosened his hold. Barely.

"Hey, what's wrong? I did ask Lea if you were cool with this and she said you were. What are you doing?" She asked and wiggled again sending all of his blood to the last place on earth that needed it.

Terrence hissed in a breath and Daisy stilled immediately as she felt what her wiggling was doing to him.

For the love of! Grrr, think of something else dammit.

"I heard a crash and thought you injured yourself. Stay right here. No. Don't move. I'll get that," he growled and gently shoved her behind him while he made quick work of the barrel and shards of pottery.

"Wow, you must be really strong," she said her voice holding a fair amount of awe and he realized he'd moved too quickly nearly giving himself away in the process.

He was just so amped up he was using way too much of his Vampire strength and agility in front of her. Did it matter though if he was going to claim her anyway?

That was the question, he supposed.

"It's just the adrenaline. Look, what are you doing up here? It's freezing."

"I know," she smiled at him and it was like the sun coming out.

"Come here, let me show you," she reached for his hand.

Without caring about the consequences, Terrence accepted her touch knowing full well he was reaching the point of no return. She was like the best kind of drug to him. Sweet and addictive. If he did not break ties now, he wouldn't be able to.

Fuck. He exhaled as he followed her into the newly erected wooden structure with thick glass panes for the roof and walls. A real greenhouse. On his roof. In Manhattan.

Whoa.

Inside were rows and rows of seedlings he couldn't possibly name. Brightly colored flowers hung from baskets. A few herbs and vegetable plants too. Along the ceiling and floors were humidifiers, misters, large lights, and heaters.

It was incredible. An entire ecosystem in a little glass box. Wondrous. Fascinating. Precious.

Like her.

"Wow," was all he could say.

"I know, right?" She smiled and he could sense her pride and happiness. His own grin echoed hers. He couldn't help it. She should always smile.

"You should have asked me first though, Daisy. I don't know if this is up to code," he said hesitating to break her joy.

"But Leandra said it would be okay," she bit her lip and stepped closer.

"I tell you what. Let me do a little looking around. Check the safety of the roof before you come up here again. Would that work for you?"

"For insurance purposes?" She asked stepping closer still.

"Sure," he agreed, but he wasn't really paying

attention to what he was agreeing too. She was so close to him and then, she moved in further.

Bold. That was a new word to describe her. He wasn't sure if he liked it. Hadn't decided what to do about her yet. But one thing was certain, if she came any closer to him, Terrence wouldn't be able to help himself.

"What are you doing?" he breathed the question more than spoke it.

"Who me?" She whispered into the dimly lit room. There was barely enough space for the two of them to stand, but he liked it that way. Liked having her close.

Terrence swallowed. She was so near now. Her soft breasts pressed against his hard chest. He felt them as if she were standing there in the nude despite the thick sweater she wore.

"You," he whispered back, his breath mingling with her.

A slow, wicked grin spread across her face. She placed her hands flat against his chest, sliding them slowly upwards until they gripped his collar. Then she pulled.

"This," she said and mashed her sweet mouth to his.

Terrence held his breath for just one moment.

He wanted to feel nothing but her lips. The softness, the steadily building pressure. He wanted to savor it, to imprint it on his memory.

This was it. The very moment when he decided what the rest of his life would be. He could push her away, excuse himself, pack his apartment up and leave town. He could spare her all of the disbelief and possible anguish of finding out that the unthinkable really did walk beside her on this very planet.

Or he could breathe. He could inhale all the earthy freshness of her scent, explore the depths of her mouth as she wanted him to. He could bite her. Swallow her blood, let it slide down his throat, solidifying their bond for eternity.

Making decisions was never his strong suit. Terrence sometimes took hours deciding what tie to wear with what shirt. How could he decide his future and hers in mere seconds?

As if she felt his internal struggle, Daisy moaned softly and pressed herself more fully against him. She'd chosen him with that small action, whether she realized it or not. Then the dam broke.

Wave after wave of torrential emotion poured throughout Terrence. The foremost being desire.

His gums ached, his throat burned, and his chest heaved. He wanted her. Now.

With a growl he grabbed her by the hips and backed her up against the wall. She clung to his lip, opening for him and thrusting her tongue into his mouth without reservation.

Terrence barely held onto himself. He wrestled control of the kiss from her searching lips. Needing to lead the pleasurable duel in order to keep his baser instincts at bay.

With one hand anchoring her soft frame to his much taller and harder one Terrence couldn't help the natural urge to flex his hips into her. Her reciprocal moan encouraged him to do it again. With his other hand around her neck and face, he tilted her head back and plundered her warm mouth more deeply.

She tasted sweet and inviting. Like the honey she'd had with her tea that morning. So good. So real. So his.

"Mmm," she held onto his shoulders. He lifted her in his arms, wanting her closer still and she complied. Lifting her legs until they were circling his waist. Her hot core pressed more fully against the ridge of his desire.

It occurred to him he'd been right when he'd

called her bold. She was. That and so much more. His body throbbed with need as they kissed and kissed and kissed some more.

Fuck. She was so goddamn irresistible. Her curvy form was the perfect foil for him. His Vampire's body was hard and svelte. Muscles corded his long frame much like a professional soccer player.

He was tall, lean, and impossibly strong. Certainly more than capable of cradling this sexy siren against him without breaking a sweat. And he had no intention of letting her go.

"Daisy," he said her name, trailing his lips down her throat and nipping her collar bone.

"I don't know about you," she whispered against his mouth, "but I'd like to continue this downstairs. In my apartment."

CHAPTER FIVE

Daisy had little experience with men. Especially a six-foot plus drop-dead gorgeous man. But something had happened in the last few days.

She hadn't quite felt herself lately. Not since she had met Terrence Davies, director, sexy nerd, mystery man and hot as fuck neighbor.

She had no idea what had come over her, but the truth was, she hadn't been able to stop thinking about her seemingly shy landlord since she'd first laid eyes on him.

Imagine her shock when he'd come storming through the door to the roof just moments ago, ripping it off its hinges actually, to find her there.

He looked so hot with his pressed khakis and

his thick cotton rugby shirt. Today's shoes were light blue with navy and yellow paisley socks. He barely seemed disheveled after his herculean display.

Even his short reddish blonde hair was perfectly combed. Like he was daring her to come closer to mess him up properly.

Challenge accepted. As if she were being maneuvered by some grand puppeteer, she'd walked over to him and to her own great surprise, she kissed him. It was touch and go for moments after that. He seemed frozen in place and Daisy almost died of embarrassment when he didn't reach for her immediately.

But something encouraged her to hold on, so she did. Lips pressed to his thin, hard and totally sexy mouth, she held onto his collar like a lifeline. Then the most wonderful thing happened.

Terrence Davies, shy hottie from next door, attacked her lips and tongue with all the suave confidence and technique of a closet Casanova.

Holy shit.

Her panties practically melted off her body with the intensity of his kiss. It was like he was trying to devour her, and yes, she was so ready to let him.

She had never done this before. *Literally never*. She was not one to jump into bed with her new neighbor, hot or not, but here she was suggesting they move this to a more comfortable place than her cold and wet greenhouse. Like her bed.

Yes. Please.

It was like some alter ego had taken over. Some secret carnal lust filled she-demon. And Daisy kind of liked it.

So there they were. Making out like two teenagers on her used sofa. Half-dressed and panting as they kissed, fondled, and rubbed all over one another. It was too fast. It was too crazy. But it felt so good she didn't want to stop.

Couldn't find any reason to. None at all. She just wanted to feel and feel and feel. And he felt so good, so right. Never before had she felt such a desperate need. Her pussy clenched on air. Her needy clit twitched and throbbed. She'd had oodles of experience touching herself, but she'd never wanted another's hands on her so damn bad. She was ready to beg.

Daisy sucked in a breath as his mouth caught her nipple through the functional cotton bra she wore beneath her shirt. She was a practical kind of girl. If he wanted lace and silk, he wasn't going to find it in her underwear drawer.

Hopefully that wouldn't be a deal breaker because for the first time in her life she was ready to have sex. With him. Now.

"Fuck, Daisy, you're so beautiful," he groaned while opening her jeans and tugging them down.

She thought about sucking in, trying to tame her belly, but quickly dismissed the notion. Forgot about it actually the very second she was completely revealed to him in all her pink cotton glory.

"You have too many clothes on," she said trying to lighten the mood.

Was that okay? Talking while attacking your neighbor? Must be she figured, because he remedied the issue by immediately shucking his own clothing and tossing it onto the floor. Daisy salivated while she took him in.

She'd seen naked men on television and once by accident in college. But that was nothing compared to the specimen before her. He stood tall and proud, his thick, long erection jutting forward more beautiful than any of those Greek statues she'd studied in school. He was like a god come to life. Her own personal *David*.

"I think we're still a little uneven," he said, his voice deep and gravelly as he dropped to his knees in front of her.

Gulp.

"I'm going to take this off you now," he said and tugged on the straps of her bra.

With a single flick of his fingers he had her bare-breasted and gasping before him like a virgin sacrifice. Which she supposed, she was.

Daisy bit her lip. She knew she was larger than most women and it wasn't necessarily a great thing. Real boobs did not stand up. They hung down. They had veins. They were functional, not picture perfect.

But he didn't seem to mind. He traced her from collar bone to nipple. Circling her sensitive flesh until finally covering her mounds. No one had ever looked at her or touched her quite like that.

"Beautiful. Perfect," he said and leaned forward to lick and suckle her hot flesh.

Daisy moaned. Her eyes wide as he tended her breasts. She never felt anything like the warm, tugging sensation that seemed to spark pleasurable little spikes straight through her body directly to her throbbing sex.

Swirl, lick, kiss, bite. Every touch, every caress,

every sweet stinging nip of his teeth on her skin made her pussy weep with longing.

"Want you, Terrence," she moaned as she leaned back granting him better access to her more than ready body.

She'd never done this before. Never had mind-numbing sex with anyone let alone a man she'd just met, but truth be told she'd felt a connection to him since the very first. He was so good looking, but it was more than that.

It was as if a light had shone down on him the first time she'd seen his silver-gray eyes. Like some ethereal force was saying, *yoo hoo Daisy this is what you've been waiting for your whole life.*

She was captivated by him. Intrigued by the ferocious spirit she'd glimpsed inside his steady gaze. Whoever Terrence Davies really was, he was a good person. True, honest, and loyal. A man she could trust. Of that she was positive.

"Are you sure you want this?"

The question startled her out of her lusty haze. She searched his face for any sign he was trying to back out but found none. Relieved, she felt herself nodding.

She didn't know why, but she was more than sure. Terrence was the one she'd been waiting for her whole life. All those lonely nights, forgotten in this one moment in his arms.

She trusted him. Knew instinctively that he would never hurt her. Wanted to join with him more than anything else.

Forever.

The thought shocked her. It was absurd. This was surely not going to be more than a one night *or afternoon* stand, but still, she wasn't going to stop.

"Yes."

One word. That was it. Three little letters that would change her life as she knew it. This wasn't about a new apartment or a new start for her business. It wasn't about the move to New York City.

This was about finally living life to its fullest. This one act meant she was finally ready to embrace and claim her life. A chance for a whole new outlook on the world for Daisy.

She was determined to grab life with two hands while she still could. Daisy wasn't that sickly, scared little girl anymore. The one whose parents sent her away to boarding school to distance themselves from their only daughter whose fragile health was too great for them to risk their affections.

It had been years since she thought about the sad childhood she'd had as a result of a genetic heart condition. Years since she'd allowed it to stop her from doing the things she wanted to. It would not stop her now. No matter how hard the organ pumped and pushed as Terrence kissed her to heights she'd never experienced before in her life.

Her life. It was her life and she was going to claim it as her own here and now. With him.

"Yes," she repeated more firmly, "I want this."

CHAPTER SIX

Terrence could hardly hear past the one word. Everything inside of him wanted to take care, to treat her gently like she deserved, but he couldn't hold himself back any more than he could hold back the progress of time.

"Need you," he murmured as he pressed her knees open and slipped his head between her soft, smooth thighs.

He kissed the tender skin up, up, up still until his lips met the thin cotton barrier that shielded his prize. With his teeth, he tore the panties from her sex, ears swallowing her moans surely as he was about to suckle her sweet cream from her most secret place.

"Mine," he growled.

Terrence dipped his tongue between her folds, lapping at her nether lips like a man starved. And he was. A starving, desperate, needy thing all for his sweet Daisy.

The mewling noises she made encouraged him to move faster, harder against her tight little bundle of nerves. The more he sucked, the harder she bucked until she was riding his face the way she would soon ride his cock. He couldn't wait to witness that.

His sweet Daisy naked as the day she entered the world, breasts bouncing, eyes wide as he thrust beneath her. Sinking into her sweet pussy was about the best damn thing he could ever imagine. She probably thought it was just this one time, but he had plans to keep her there forever. To be his one and only for as long as the gods and Fates allowed.

Time slowed as he lapped at her sex. He pressed closer between her legs, parting her nether lips with his fingers to better taste her essence. Terrence's large shoulders spread her thighs even further apart, making more room for him while he made love to her with lips, teeth, and tongue.

The ripples of her first orgasm began to build sending trembling waves echoing through him as he continued to kiss and suckle her sweet cream lick by delicious lick.

Her emotions screamed at him, he realized as he read her needs one by one. She liked what he was doing. Wanted him to continue. And he intended to.

Daisy's submission to his touch made Terrence wild with need. As he kissed her sweet pussy, he added first one then another finger, stretching her tight sheath to the limit. She was so small.

Holy shit. The reason for her tightness made itself known as he pumped his fingers into her slick heat. That male part of him wanted to roar and thump his chest. His little mate was untried! A virgin.

Fucking perfect and mine. She was so beautiful. So new to all this. It almost hurt him to touch her this way, but he couldn't stop. Not now. He wanted, no he needed to be part of her. Right then and there.

He vowed to make it good for her. It was his privilege as her mate. And he was. Born to love this one woman forever forsaking all others.

"Oh my God," she yelled, clutching at his hair as she came apart under the onslaught of his ministrations. On and on it went. The pulsing, throbbing need burning throughout her mind, heart and body and flowing into him making his cock pulse with pure undiluted desire.

Fuck. She felt so good, squeezing his fingers. He couldn't wait until she was doing the same to his cock. To be the first to love her, the only man to love her, that was his ultimate wish. But first he needed to explain.

"Daisy," he growled her name as her sex clenched around his fingers one last time.

"Please," she said sitting up and clawing at him until his face was level with hers, "don't you dare stop."

Terrence growled. She tried his patience sorely. All he wanted was to thrust away, but he would never do anything to harm her. Careful as he could he lifted her from the couch and walked with her to the bedroom.

This was as sacred a moment as he'd ever experienced in his almost three centuries on the Earth. He eased her down, following her with his body.

"Daisy," he said kissing her lips as he placed the head of his cock against her entrance.

"Yes," she gasped aloud and Terrence swallowed the sound as he slowly pushed into her tight heat.

The desperation he saw in her eyes matched his own. She needed him as much as he needed her.

"Daisy, love. I am sorry this is going to hurt."

"Don't be. I was waiting for you," she said astounding him with her frankness.

"Hold on, *bellissima*," he groaned as he pushed against the barrier of her virginity, stilling at once when he felt her tense.

He hoped to kiss away the pain that flashed briefly in her eyes. A scant moment, but one that he would feel to his soul. But he would make up for it. His bond with his mate already more real than he'd ever believed it could be.

It was as if he were on fire and she was his only salvation. He pressed deep, meeting the barrier of her innocence with trepidation. He'd never taken a woman's virginity before. This was new and scary. Exciting in a way that could only mean they were truly meant for each other.

Fate had given him a true gift. One he would treasure forever. Daisy groaned as he penetrated her long and deep. He winced, feeling the pain through their weak though present bond. That burning pain of him stretching her was almost finished. His possession almost complete.

One more push and they both groaned in relief. Finally. She was his.

Tendrils of magic wove around them and Terrence hissed against her neck. Gasping for air, he retreated slightly to seat himself even more fully inside her hot, tight core.

This was the beginning of it all. The start of something so deep and magical it defied reason. Together, they set a new rhythm. She clamped her legs around him and he leaned down mashing his lips to hers.

In and out, deep thrust and shallow retreat. His tongue echoed the movements of his cock as he became one with his mate in a communion of bodies and souls as old as time. Each move was a line in a song, each sigh a note in a symphony.

She was, in a word, sublime.

A nymph in her magical garden ten stories up in the coldest month of the year and the busiest city in the world. Unreachable. Unattainable. Yet his. All his. Only his.

"Daisy," he said her name as he pressed his lips to hers.

Wide emerald eyes glittered with passion and pleasure as he seesawed in and out of her heat. His fangs pressed against his gums, the needlelike teeth threatening to descend, but he kept them in check. For now.

This was too big, too substantial a moment. Terrence was introducing Daisy to what it meant to truly be a Vampire's lover. He wanted it to be good. Hell, he wanted it to be so fucking good she would never want to let him go.

Fuck. Terrence gripped the pillow behind her head. Afraid he would harm her with his hold he felt the material give way as clouds of feathers now filled the room.

His hips propelled in and out of her tight sheath. So desperate to reach that pinnacle, to find release within her warm, lush body, he groaned as he lost himself inside her. Inside the heaven she promised. A kind of salvation for him, and untold pleasures for certain.

Daisy's body jerked and shivered beneath him. He let out a groan as her pussy squeezed his cock. The beginnings of her second orgasm started to ripple through her, egging on his own release.

His fangs threatened to burst forth, the need to quench his desire for her blood rose inside of him.

Claim. Mate. The mantra played over and over in his head like a separate minded beast of its own. Yes, he was there in the moment. Completely captivated by the way she generously and wholeheartedly gave her innocence to him.

Her submission was a gift. Her body a wonder of dips and curves, valleys and secret places that he couldn't wait to explore and memorize.

"Terrence," she whispered, eyes wide, glistening with unshed tears as the swell of bliss began to flow between them.

Watching her come was like witnessing something unearthly, something divine. The pleasure she unabashedly took from him spurred on his own release.

Claim her now, the thought screamed in his brain. His gums ached with the descension of his fangs. The exchange of bodily fluids was needed. Three to be exact.

Three life-giving liquids needed to be given and taken between a Vampire and his *sete di cuore* for the mating to be complete.

She would fulfill his longing, quench his heart's thirst as no one else in the universe could. And he would in turn share with her his strength, his healing abilities, and his extended lifespan.

Three fluids exchanged. That was all that was required. That would be the culmination of their mating.

Saliva from their lips, *cum from their bodies*, and lastly, *blood from their veins*. He just needed to complete the last step.

"Yes," she answered his unspoken question.

"I haven't asked you yet, Daisy. You don't know what it is I want of you," he gasped as the pleasure spiked.

"It doesn't matter. Whatever it is, I choose you. My answer is yes, yes!" She moaned deep and long as her walls contracted around him. Her pussy milked him, sucking the seed from his cock until he bellowed in blissful agony.

His hunger unbearable. Terrence looked into her wide green eyes then he struck. His needlelike teeth sunk into the soft skin of her neck to drink from the vein that fed her heart.

Terrence moaned in delight as he sipped from her flesh. Sweet and flowery like her scent, her blood tingled on his tongue before gliding down his throat and filling him with the most peace he had ever felt.

She sighed and moaned against him, her second orgasm making it all the more pleasurable as he licked her wounds closed.

"Daisy," he moaned her name, thrusting one more time until he was no longer able to move.

His heart thundered and he tried to catch his breath while snuggling her close. He listened to her own racing heart and it calmed him slightly. Terrence was aware something very profound had just happened.

Something that would either be his making or his undoing. Breathing heavily still, he savored her essence on his lips.

She was inside of him now. By drinking her blood he would always know her feelings, feel her emotions, be closer to her than any other individual on the planet.

The sacred bond was almost complete. He just had to give her some of his blood. But first, they needed to talk.

Shit. Terrence hated talking. He'd much rather stick his nose in a book or in music.

He was an excellent director because he'd been around a very long time. People watching was a hobby. He knew how they moved. How they reacted to different stimuli. It gave him an advantage wen setting the stage.

But he couldn't predict this. He couldn't predict what Daisy would say when he dropped this particular bomb on her.

"That was, I mean. Wow," she sighed and nuzzled his chest.

Pride made him want to thump his chest and roar to the world, but instead he squeezed her close. Loving the feel of her lush curves against the hard planes of his body.

"Are you okay?" He asked, suddenly afraid he had drunk too much.

"Yes. I am fantastic," she smiled and kissed his chest.

"We need to talk," he repeated again on a moan. Damn she was amazing. Everything about her called to him. The way she touched him made him want to be balls deep inside her all over again.

But first.

"About what?"

"Well, there is something I need to tell you."

"Oh. You mean that you're a Vampire?"

Terrence went completely still. Eyes wide he looked down at the mischievous expression on her face and opened his mouth only to close it again.

"How did? When? Why didn't you say something?"

CHAPTER SEVEN

"Okay first of all, you just bit my neck, buddy. I might have been a virgin up till a few minutes ago, but I'm not an idiot," Daisy sat up completely unembarrassed by her nudity.

She was a big girl, but clearly her Vampire lover did not mind. Not if the way he'd kissed, sucked, and nibbled all her pink bits meant anything. And damn, but she was sure it did.

Was it possible to fall in love at first *bite*? She certainly had done just that. Why else would she have given herself fully to a virtual stranger?

"So, I have some questions first, okay?" She asked.

"Okay," he said cautiously.

"Do you drink other people's blood?"

"No. Uh, actually I get most of my blood from a specialty butcher."

"Animal blood? Isn't that weird?"

"No stranger than eating a steak, but now, I mean I don't want to presume, but if you choose to remain with me I am hoping to close that account," he said in a rather shy voice she found endearing.

"Ah. I see," she smiled and snuggled into his chest loving the way he wrapped his strong arms around her and kissed on the top of her head.

No doubt about it. Daisy Amante was head over heels for this sexy, nerdy Vampire. No, she hadn't disclosed her health issues yet, but that was alright. She'd had a good report at her last check-up. It would be okay.

Damn straight, she thought to herself. The universe would have a lot to answer for if it finally gave her a piece of happiness only to take it away.

"Are you okay with this, Daisy?"

"I knew what you were before you bit me, Terrence. I am more than okay."

He sat straight up almost knocking her to the floor with the sudden movement. Of course, he caught her before she could fall off the bed.

"When? When did you know?"

"Well, I knew you were too damn good looking to be a *normal*, but I was thinking more along the lines of Werewolf myself."

"What? How do you know about them?"

"I don't know. Well, no that's not true. You see, my grandmother had the gift of sight. It skips a generation or so I am told. My mom doesn't have it. Unfortunately, that's not all I got from her," she sat up and tried to distance herself from him, but his arms wrapped around her and his eyes furrowed as if he didn't like the idea of her moving away one bit. The thought warmed her.

"Tell me everything," he said in that deep gravelly voice she'd come to love. *So serious.*

"Okay, so I was born with the ability to sense certain things. The first time I ran into the supernatural world I was three and a bad Witch tried to give me a poisoned apple. Ridiculously cliché, I know. Anyway I screamed for my grandma and she outed the woman to the local Coven who had her sent away."

"Wow, that is incredible," he murmured nodding for her to continue.

"Anyway, after that Grandma kind of told me things a bit at a time. She got sick when I was ten and passed away soon after. That was when my parents discovered I had inherited the same bad heart that killed my grandmother. They shipped me off to boarding school afterwards and I pretty much stayed to myself except for Leandra."

"And your gift?"

"Oh, she doesn't know. It's not very strong or clear, my gift that is, but I use it to stay out of trouble. In fact, I never told anyone except you."

"I see," he said nodding.

"Are you angry? Because of my condition?"

Daisy waited for him to scream or push her away. True, he was the first man she'd been intimate with, but she'd dated others. Every time she thought she could tell them about her heart, it turned out bad.

Most men didn't want to date a girl with a premature expiration date. It was kind of like buying milk past its due date one guy friend had said. *Sigh.*

"Look at me, Daisy," Terrence tipped her head up and looked at her with those glittering silver eyes of his.

She loved his face. He had impossibly high cheekbones, a strong chin, and slightly crooked nose. Of course, his full lips were amazing. And the smattering of thick, copper eyelashes that brushed his cheeks whenever he opened and closed his eyes.

"Daisy?"

"Sorry," she blushed and turned her attention back to what he was saying.

"I know it seems too soon for this, but I love you. All of you. You've given me an incredible gift."

"My virginity?"

At that he laughed and pulled her close, kissing her on the head before taking her face in his hands in continuing.

"Yes, there is that, but I was talking about your acceptance. As for your heart, it doesn't matter. You see, my love, you are my *sete di cuore*. The one person in the world my heart thirsts for. I never thought I would meet anyone like you."

"What a twenty-nine-year old virgin?" She laughed.

"No, a beautiful woman with the ability to make a wonderland grow in the middle of a steel and brick city in winter."

"Terrence, you say the most amazing things," she bit her lip waiting for him to finish so she could move on to better things. Like kissing him.

"You see, I didn't think I was worthy."

"Why wouldn't you be worthy?"

"I had a friend. He was bad, Daisy, he hunted normals. I called my old Coven and they called the Guardians. He was thrown in jail, but I felt as if I had failed him and the others. I left the Coven and have been on my own since then."

"I am sure they don't blame you," she said her heart hurting for him.

"Doesn't matter now. It's been a very long time. But you see, I thought I would always be alone. Then you showed up and I started to believe again. To hope."

"There you go again," she said, leaning into him. God his lips were so close, so tempting.

"I need you, Daisy. I love you. I want you to be mine."

"Yes," she sighed as she pressed her mouth to his. It sounded good to her.

He broke the kiss and pierced his wrist with his teeth. Daisy bent her head to the warm red liquid and began to drink from him.

She expected it to be gross or metallic, but it wasn't. Not at all.

Terrence's blood was hot and spicy. Like expensive chocolate laced with cayenne. Rich and flavorful, it colored her palate and made her hungry for more of him.

Suddenly, she felt hot and dropped his wrist. Terrence held her loosely as she fell against him. Something was happening. Something she had no idea how to control. So instead, she let go. Daisy gasped, back arching as liquid fire seemed to flow through her.

Her limbs ached, heart squeezed, and gums throbbed. When it stopped, she turned to him with her new fangs and smiled.

"Daisy?" He said and watched as understanding flowed between their bond.

"I didn't realize," he murmured tracing her new deadly additions carefully with his finger.

"I did," she said and pulled his head down to hers.

"I love you, mate," he breathed into her mouth as he kissed her.

Daisy turned around feeling ten times as strong as before. She was more than ready to make love to her one true mate, her own *sete di cuore* again. This time their bond would make it even better than before.

"I love you too," she moaned as she lowered herself down on his thick hard cock.

She rocked her hips, taking him deeper and more fully than their first time.

"Will it always be like this?" She asked as her belly tightened with the promise of ecstasy as tendrils of familiar pleasure began in her core.

"Better, my love," Terrence groaned and grabbed her hips. He guided her, lifted her up and down capturing her nipple in his mouth as they sought heaven in each other's arms.

Many long, wonderful minutes later as they laid in a twist of limbs and sheets. Daisy listened to his heartbeat and sighed, happier than she had ever felt in her entire life.

"Happy?" He asked.

"I am. Deliriously so," she replied.

EPILOGUE

"What's going on?"

Terrence ran into the apartment amidst the construction and sought out his mate. Heart pounding he was glad to find her unharmed puttering away in the new larger and safer greenhouse that he'd had built directly above their combined apartment.

In fact, he'd had the entire top floor of his building redone to suit them both. Making one huge apartment out of two was something of a feat but adding a long spiral staircase that lead to the new greenhouse was something else.

His mate had loved it of course. And he lived for making her happy.

"Terrence?"

"Something happened when I was at work. I felt it."

He watched as a becoming blush spread across his mate's beautiful face. She looked good enough to eat in her baggy sweatshirt and black leggings.

He stepped closer cradling her face in his hands and wiping the small smudge of dirt from her cheek affectionately. Now that he knew she was unharmed he could breathe again though his curiosity had not diminished.

"When did the crew leave?"

"About an hour ago," she answered sighing into him as she always did. So accepting. So beautiful. So sweet it hurt.

"What made your blood pressure spike not so long ago, love?"

"Oh that," she tried to evade the question by reaching on tiptoes and thrusting her tongue in his mouth. He scented her desire, his own body hardening in response.

Terrence would always want her. His desire grew every day. She was his *sete di cuore*. It would always be this way, but first he needed to know.

"Do you know how you reached out to the Coven to explain your turning me?"

"Yes. We went to see Dr. Lively last week. Did something happen with your blood tests?"

"No. Yes." She giggled and covered her face with her hands.

"Well, it seems that even though instances of turning are exceedingly rare they do happen. I am now a Vampire like you and, well, I'm pregnant!"

"What?" Terrence was completely dumbfounded.

Sure, he had been born a Vampire. It was a mutation after all. But he had no idea he could pass it on to his mate. And he had no idea said mate could bear offspring.

"They want me to come in for more tests next week, but Terrence, I feel great!"

He was so chocked he could hardy speak. First a mate, now young. Was it really true?

"Wait, are you not happy?" Daisy asked, eyes wide with uncertainty.

What the fuck are you doing? Say something, idiot! He scolded himself. Without waiting another second, he scooped up his mate and held her to him.

"So you are happy?" She laughed and nuzzled his neck, scraping over his newly acquired mate mark with her fine pointed teeth.

"You have given me more than I could have hoped for," he said and he meant it.

"I love you," she said.

"I love you too. Forever," he returned.

"Forever? Show me then," her eyes flashed with her demand and Terrence used all his supernatural skill and grace to get them to their bedroom safely and quickly.

"I will never stop showing you how much I love you," Terrence said.

He slowly undressed his sweet Daisy. His mate. Revealing her pale perfection one inch at a time to his greedy silver gaze.

So perfect and all his.

He took his time proving his point about loving her forever until she was hoarse from crying out. Then he did it all over again.

The end.

Liked this story? Read More Purely Paranormal Romance Books by C.D. Gorri by clicking here!

GRIZZLY LOVER

Teresa broke Oliver's heart once before, but now she needs his help. Can her Grizzly lover put the past behind them?

Oliver Pax is one of the most prolific composers of all time. He is the award-winning writer of such Broadway hits as The Beast of Brooklyn Heights and its upcoming conclusion Where Beauty Lives. A loner known for his grumpy and secretive nature, the reclusive Grizzly Bear Shifter is in for the shock of his life when a blast from his past washes up on his doorstep after a terrible accident.

Teresa Witherspoon has been on the run for the past two years. She's traveled across the country and back again fearing the day her father and his henchmen find her and her son. Caring for Thomas has kept her going this far, but when an accident leaves her hospitalized, she has no choice but to call the one person she swore to stay away from.

Will the Grizzly Bear Shifter she'd once loved help her in her time of need?

Liked this story? Read More Purely Paranormal Romance Books by C.D. Gorri by clicking here!

READING ON A BUDGET?

BUY DIRECT GET 30% OFF

Hello Readers!

I am so excited to be able to offer you exclusive bundles available only on CDGORRI.COM for readers using my BUY DIRECT option.

Right now, I have several bundles available at a whopping 30% off the listed prices and there are several series bundles to choose from.

Orders will be delivered via BookFunnel email. Just download to your favorite app and READ!

Thank you for buying direct. Have an awesome day!

xoxo,

C.D. Gorri

BEWARE... HERE BE DRAGONS!

The Falk Clan Tales began as my stories surrounding four dragon Brothers and how they find their one true mates, but when a long lost brother arrives on the scene, followed by a few more Shifters...what can I say? The more the merrier!

Each Dragon's chest is marked with his rose, the magical link to his heart and his magic. They each have a matching gemstone to go with it.

She's given up on love. But he's just begun.
In The Dragon's Valentine we meet the eldest Falk brother, Callius. He is on a mission to find a

Castle and his one true mate, one he can trust with his diamond rose....

His heart is frozen. Can she change his mind about love?

In The Dragon's Christmas Gift our attention shifts to Alexsander, the youngest brother of the four. He has resigned himself to a life alone, until he meets *her*.

Some wounds run deep. Can a Dragon's heart be unbroken?

The Dragon's Heart is the story of Edric Falk who has vowed never to love again, but that changes when he meets his feisty mate, Joselyn Curacao.

She just wants a little fun. He's looking for a lifetime.

We finally meet Nikolai Falk and his sexy Shifter mate in The Dragon's Secret.

She doesn't believe in fairytales, until a Dragon comes knocking on her door.

Meet Castor Falk, the long lost brother of our original four Dragons, and his sassy mate Josette.

The Dragon's Treasure is full of adventure and laughs.

Nothing can surprise this six hundred-year-old Dragon, except maybe her.

Devine Graystone meets his match in Sunny Daye, an irrepressible Wolf Shifter with a heart of gold. Read their story in The Dragon's Surprise.

He's a hardcore realist until she dares him to dream.

Nicholas Gravestone doesn't know what to think when he spies Minerva Lykos on the property his Dragon covets. Can this unlikely pair come to a truce? Find out in The Dragon's Dream.

Thanks for reading.

xoxo,

C.D. Gorri

*Dragon Mates & Dragon Mates 2 boxed sets are now available in hardcover, paperback, and ebook.

ALSO BY C.D. GORRI

Contemporary Romance Books:

Cherry On Top Tales

Her Yule His Log

His Carrot Her Muffin

Her Chocolate His Bar

Wild Billionaire Romance

His Wild Obsession

Jersey Bad Boys

Merciful Lies

***

Paranormal Romance Books:

Macconwood Pack Novel Series:

Macconwood Pack Tales Series:

The Falk Clan Tales:

The Bear Claw Tales:

The Barvale Clan Tales:

Barvale Holiday Tales:

Purely Paranormal Romance Books:

The Wardens of Terra:

The Maverick Pride Tales:

Dire Wolf Mates:

Wyvern Protection Unit:

Jersey Sure Shifters/EveL Worlds:

The Guardians of Chaos:

Twice Mated Tales

Hearts of Stone Series

Moongate Island Tales

Mated in Hope Falls

Speed Dating with the Denizens of the Underworld

Hungry Fur Love

Island Stripe Pride

NYC Shifter Tales

A Howlin' Good Fairytale Retelling

Standalones:

Witch Shifter Clan

Young Adult/Urban Fantasy Books

The Grazi Kelly Novel Series

The Angela Tanner Files

G'Witches Magical Mysteries Series

Co-written with P. Mattern

Witches of Westwood Academy

with Gina Kincade

Blackthorn Academy For Supernaturals

**Be sure to check out my BUY DIRECT BUNDLES* and get 30% off when you buy available only my website.*

ABOUT THE AUTHOR

USA Today Bestselling author C.D. Gorri writes paranormal and contemporary romance and urban fantasy books with plenty of steam and humor.

Join her mailing list here: https://www.cdgorri.com/newsletter

An avid reader with a profound love for books and literature, she is usually found with a book in hand. C.D. lives in her home state, New Jersey, where many of her characters and stories are based. Her tales are fast-paced yet detailed with satisfying conclusions. If you enjoy powerful heroines and loyal heroes who face relatable problems in supernatural settings, journey into the Grazi Kelly Universe today.

You will find sassy, curvy heroines and sexy, love-driven heroes who find their HEAs between the pages.

Wolves, Bears, Dragons, Tigers, Witches, Vampires, and tons more Shifters and supernatural creatures dwell within her paranormal works. The most important thing is every mate in this universe is fated, loyal, and true lovers always get their happily-ever-afters.

In her contemporary works, you will find fiercely possessive men and the smart, confident, curvy women they are crazy about. As always, the HEA is between the pages.

Thank you and happy reading!
 del mare alla stella,
 C.D. Gorri

http://www.cdgorri.com
 https://www.facebook.com/Cdgorribooks
 https://www.bookbub.com/authors/c-d-gorri
 https://twitter.com/cgor22
 https://instagram.com/cdgorri/

https://www.goodreads.com/cdgorri
https://www.tiktok.com/@cdgorriauthor3